Dedicated to Henry and Samuel

GRUMPY FOX

Follow us on instagram @grumpyfoxbooks

Text and illustrations copyright © Ben Hunter 2022.

Every evening when Henry and Sam were asleep,

Into the kitchen something did creep,

And ate their last biscuit.

It didn't ask, it just nicked it.

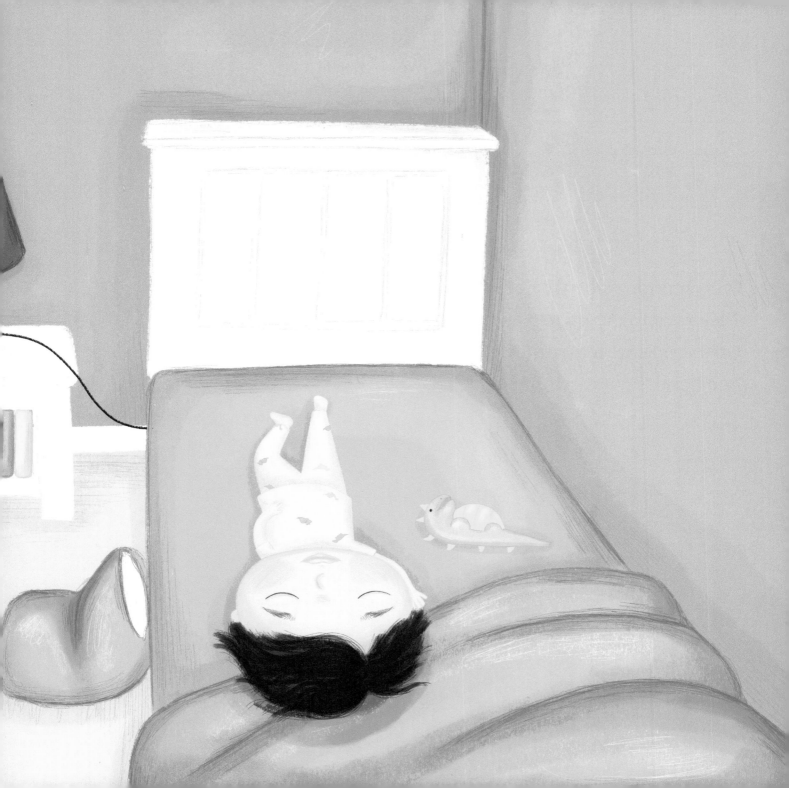

Every morning when the boys came downstairs,

They went to the kitchen and shouted "this isn't fair!

On the side, we left one Rich Tea.

And now it's gone – who could it be?"

It happened every single night.
They woke up to such a fright.
Whilst they were in bed dreaming sweet dreams,
Something had eaten all of their custard creams.

"It must be a monster" said Sam (the youngest of the brothers).
"He ate all our biscuits. Now we must buy some others."
Henry said "I bet the monster is purple and hairy
With big horns and red eyes. He must be scary."

"We must lay a trap" said Henry. "Whilst we are in bed,
We will catch the monster eating our last shortbread."
Samuel said "Or we could leave him a chocolate one.
This is going to be so much fun!"

That night the boys left a biscuit on the side

"Now the monster will have nowhere to hide."

They didn't know the monster would be so picky and selective,

And completely ignored their chocolate digestive.

The next morning, they couldn't believe their eyes.

"This certainly is a big surprise!"

They thought hard about how they could catch him,

And then said "We should leave the whole biscuit tin."

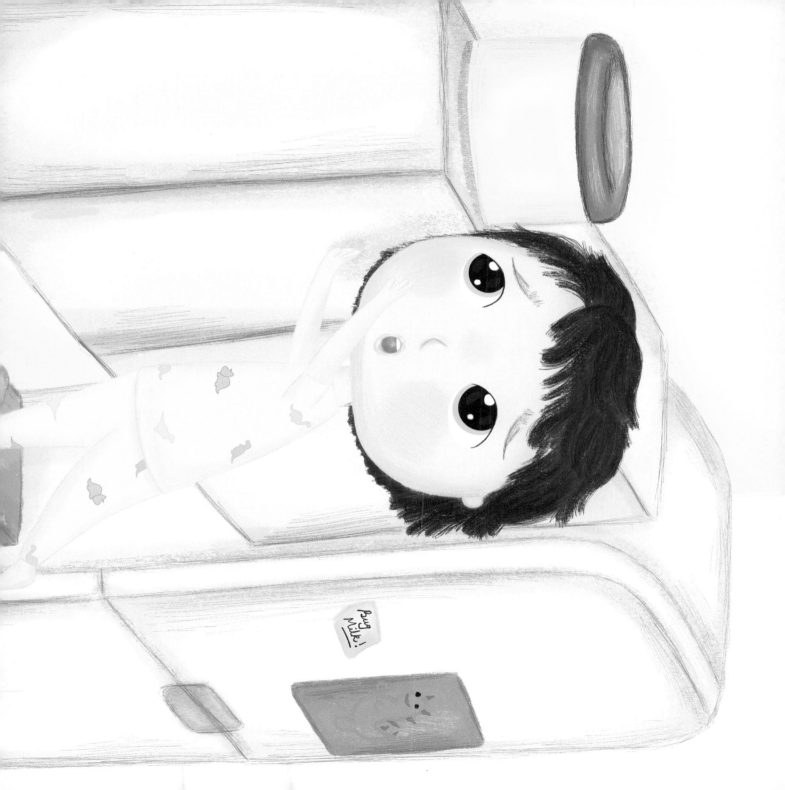

Inside the tin, was every type of biscuit you could think up,

From pink wafers, to jammy dodgers, to a cookie cup.

"This will surely catch him this time!" Henry exclaimed.

"Biscuit monster, we will get you and you will be tamed!"

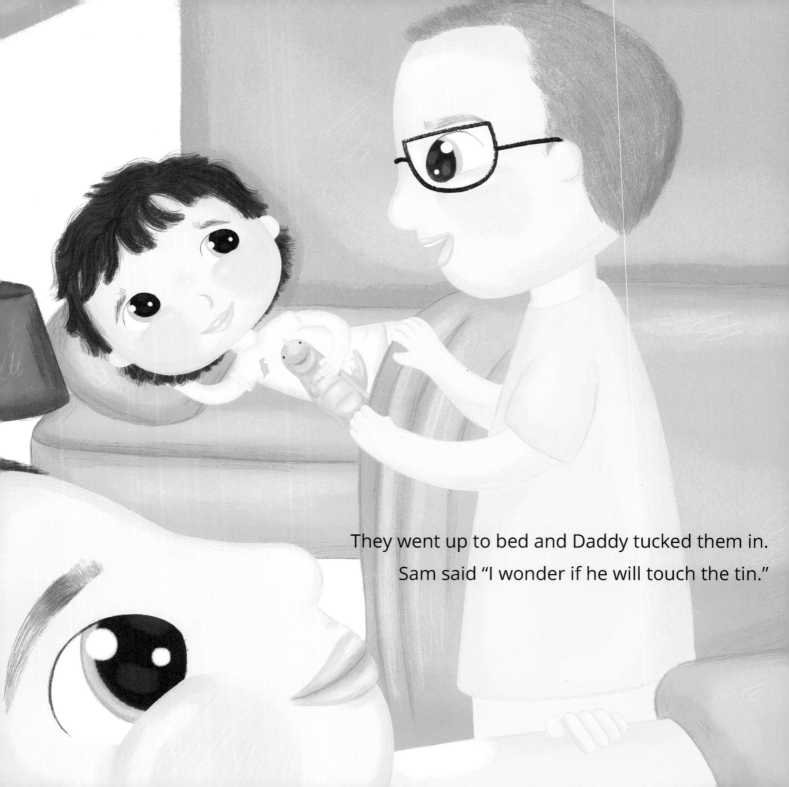

They went up to bed and Daddy tucked them in.
Sam said "I wonder if he will touch the tin."

They went to sleep and when they woke in the morning,
Daddy was standing in the kitchen yawning.

The boys had still not caught the monster but were getting suspicious.

The monster had left a note saying "Thanks for the biscuits. They were delicious."

"Why are you so tired, Daddy?" asked Sam.

Henry questioned "And why is your face covered in jam?"

To catch the thief, the boys had one final plan.

Was it a monster or was it a man?

They set up a camera to record and catch the baddy,

And watched the next morning to see it was....

DADDY!